TUR

AN ELSKER SAGA NOVELLA

S.T. BENDE

Tur
An Elsker Saga Novella
Copyright © 2013, S.T. Bende
Edited by: Eden Plantz and Stacey Nash
Cover Art by: Rebecca K. Sterling, Sterling Design Studios

ALSO BY S.T. BENDE

Meet the Vikings in VIKING ACADEMY:

VIKING ACADEMY

VIKING CONSPIRACY

VIKING VOW

Meet the Norse God of War in THE ÆRE SAGA:

PERFEKT ORDER

PERFEKT CONTROL

PERFEKT BALANCE

PERFEKT MATCH

Meet the Norse God of Winter in THE ELSKER SAGA:

ELSKER

ENDRE

TRO

TUR *(a novella)*

Meet the demigods in NIGHT WAR SAGA:

PROTECTOR

DEFENDER

REDEEMER

Complete list of S.T.'s STAR WARS *titles at*

www.stbende.com/star-wars

Stay in touch with S.T. at www.stbende.com.

And sign up for S.T.'s newsletter at

http://smarturl.it/BendeNewsletter

DEDICATION

To my adorable princes.
All your dreams can come true.

CHAPTER 1

BREATHE, *INGA. YOU'VE got this.*

An angry god was coming at me from across the clearing, legs pumping with decent speed. He was a blur of red hair and clenched fists, the visible embodiment of rage. Thick, blue veins pulsed beneath muscular forearms, and I could feel the fury seething from every pore. I managed to avoid the first series of punches, but the livid deity landed a fast uppercut that sent me flying. My ears rang as I shook my head, evicting the stars behind my eyes. It wasn't like me to miss a sucker-punch.

I jumped to my feet just in time. The god charged at me like a Celtic dancer – head down, arms at his sides. Interesting approach. I sidestepped him, but he circled around, hooking my neck with one arm and forcing me down. He pounced with outstretched hands, clearly aiming for my throat. I tucked my knees over my head so he landed face first in the dirt. He came up, spitting bark and angrier than ever.

"Good," I murmured as the god started circling. "Now I've gotcha." When he lunged again, I caught his fist between two hands. His eyes widened as I squeezed. Hard. When I heard his knuckles crack, I bent my knees and pushed off the balls of my feet. I threw my arms across my chest, hurtling my opponent off the ground. He landed on his back, the air leaving his lungs in a painful sound. I left him clutching a complete set of broken fingers.

"Nice effort, Christian." I tilted my head and offered a hand to help him up. "You nearly got me a few times there. Do you know where you went wrong?"

My student glared as he hoisted himself up with his good arm. "*Nei*. But Odin knows you're going to spell it out for me."

"It's not my idea of a good time to teach you basic combat skills on Sunday morning. You're the one who almost got himself killed in Jotunheim last week. Not me."

"That wasn't my fault, the—"

"I don't want to hear it. I don't care if they shoved stark-weed root under your fingernails and used voodoo to make you sprout a second head. Your commander asked me to get you up to speed so you don't get anyone else in your unit killed. And it's my day off. So hurry up and tell me what you did wrong."

"The guys were right about you. You're a nightmare." My charge cradled his broken hand. What a baby. While I normally enjoyed my job as Fight Choreographer and Chief Tactical Advisor for Asgard's warriors, some days, it could be a royal pain. Since Christian had neither stopped whining nor improved his attack in the past ninety minutes, this morning garnered a *royal pain* checkmark.

"Thank you. Now, tell me where you went wrong."

"Uh…" Christian glared at me. He was probably wondering how a girl just beat him at hand to hand. They were all like that the first time we worked together. Seasoned warriors cherished private sessions with me. Greenhorns loathed them.

"Where was your head two minutes ago?" I probed.

"I wanted to kill you."

"That's good. But you were coming from an emotional place. Combat's all about strategy. If you've got too much going on here," I tapped his chest, "Then you can't focus on what should be going on here." He ducked before I could tap his head. Touchy little bugger.

"Fine. Let's go again."

"Can you stay in your head this time, or do you need to cool it for a few minutes? If you're going to last more than a week at this job, you better learn to shut down your emotions. Find a little switch inside and just—" I flicked my finger in the air. "Turn it off. You have to want to kill me for the right reasons. And those reasons aren't here." I tapped his heart. Christian grimaced.

"I get it. Let's just get this over with."

"I hope you *do* get it. I need to get dinner in the oven before the Assignment Meeting, so I can't be here past eleven. Move it or lose your other hand."

"Whatever." Christian glared at me and retreated to the corner of the clearing. "On your mark."

I straightened my ponytail and dropped into a fighting stance. "Now!"

Three exhausting hours later, I swiped mascara across my lashes and put on my anniversary present from Gunnar. The diamond studs sparkled against my earlobes, so I added a touch of glittery shadow to my eyelids to set them off. A few quick strokes with my boar bristle brush and my long, blonde hair shone to perfection.

"Come on, babe. We're going to be late." Gunnar handed me the gold sash hanging over the bedpost. I glanced up and couldn't help but smile. His wild brown hair made him look like he'd just rolled out of bed, but I knew him well enough to know he'd spent a good five minutes artfully arranging each spike to frame his face.

"Why are you staring at me?" Gunnar tilted his head.

"You're just cute." I tied my sash in a loose knot around my waist. We weren't supposed to accessorize our dress robes, but they were unfortunate-looking on their own. All the riches of the realms and *this* was the best Odin could come up with? Honestly.

"I'm ready. Wait." I swiped a coat of gloss over my lips. "Now I'm ready."

Christian and his iron will had left me seriously behind schedule. I'd run all the way home, thrown my roast in the oven, taken a super short shower *without even exfoliating*, and we were still barely going to make the Assignment Meeting. But it'd been worth it. I'd left Christian singing my praises – he wouldn't be a liability to his unit any more. With a few years' practice, he might even make the Elite Team.

"Hold on. Before we leave… you have something right here." Gunnar came up from behind me. He wrapped strong arms around my waist and pulled me to his chest. It felt hard against my back, the muscles still knotted from his morning workout. I closed my eyes and breathed in his soapy smell. It was comforting and exhilarating all at once. My senses stirred as Gunnar tugged the neck of my robe down, exposing my shoulder. He brushed his lips against the muscle with a feather light touch. A thousand nerve endings performed jumping jacks with military precision.

"Oh, do I?" My head fell to the side. "What about right here?"

"There too." Gunnar kissed a trail from my shoulder to the nape of my neck. His tongue flicked against my skin, sending the aerobically gifted nerves into overdrive. They pulsed against each brush of his lips, driving a slow burn deep into my abdomen. I reached up to grip the spikes of his still-damp hair, and as I did he covered my stomach with one massive hand. He pulled me closer as he kissed me from behind. He raked my earlobe between his teeth, a decision that was sure to derail our afternoon. Who cared? This was going to be a *much* more enjoyable way to spend the day.

I whirled around so my chest pushed up against his. Gunnar palmed my behind with both hands, pulling me closer. "Have I ever told you that you have an exquisite backside?"

"I believe you once said that was why you married me," I teased.

Gunnar squeezed lightly, and my head swam from the rush of blood. In one swift movement he bent down and clothes-lined my knees so I fell into his arms. As he stalked toward the bed we heard an irate voice from the living room.

"We are late!"

Ull.

"Shove off, mate!" Gunnar yelled back. He continued his determined trajectory toward the bed.

"Wait." My fingers grazed his face. The prickly fibers of his day-old beard tickled my skin. "Odin will kill us if we miss the meeting. Then, Ull will kill us again for ticking off Odin. How many lives do you have left?"

"Who said anything about missing the meeting? I only need half an hour. He'll still be working his way through the tertiary gods by then." Gunnar gave me a look that sent tingles down my back. "You really want to stop doing this?"

"No." I stared at the emerald eyes twinkling at me. "But I also don't want to hear it from Ull for the next five years."

"Wouldn't hurt him to break one rule." Gunnar grumbled. "Scratch that. It might. Fine, doll. You win this one. But this isn't over."

"I should hope not," I stroked the stubble dusting his jaw. "Besides, you might only need half an hour. But I'm going to need more." With a wink I laced my fingers through Gunnar's. He let out a soft growl.

"Careful what you wish for. You don't know what you're getting into."

"Oh, I know *exactly* what I'm getting into." I pulled my hand away from his to smack his behind. Then I strode down the hallway, punctuating my exit with a hair toss. I heard Gunnar's laughter as I entered the living room of the house we shared with our best friend. Ull sat on the couch, muscular arms stretched across its back. His hair was in characteristic disarray, and his pale blue eyes sparkled in the early afternoon light. From a distance he was the picture of calm, but when I looked closer, I noticed his fingers tapping. He was ticked.

"About time," Ull grumbled. "We are late."

"I know." I patted his head.

"I am not your pet, Inga." Correction. Ull was *really* ticked.

"Right." My fingers moved side to side, ruffling his hair instead.

"Stop that."

Ignoring him, I crossed to the door. "Instead of being mad, you could try congratulating me. My morning student is ready to declare me fight choreographer extraordinaire, since I gave him the tools to whomp on that troll, Skadi."

"She is still acting out, I take it?" Ull stretched his long legs as he stood. At six feet five inches, he stood two inches over Gunnar, and nearly a full foot over me. He had the kind of posture typical of Elite Team warriors – shoulders back, head high. But unlike most of the warriors, Ull never let his guard down; not even at home.

"She's still fuming you won't go out with her. And arrogant as Helheim that she's the only female warrior. Is there any chance she'll go back to whatever realm she crawled out of?" I tried not to stare while Gunnar adjusted the ridiculous number of medals pinned to his uniform. He was the third highest ranking warrior in total kills, after Thor and Ull, and he had the hardware to prove it. It wasn't fair that he had to look so sexy on a day we had somewhere to be. Maybe he could keep the medals on later…

"Ull's not so secret admirer, leave Asgard? I wish." Gunnar closed the front door. "I can't wait to see Christian take her down. When do they spar next?"

"Tuesday morning." I hurried after Ull, who walked purposefully ahead of us. Rule follower that he was, he'd never been late for anything in his entire existence. "I'll be watching."

"Me too." Gunnar ran a hand through his brown spikes and raised an eyebrow at Ull. We broke into a jog to catch up.

"I hope this thing is over quickly," I took Gunnar's hand as we ran. The day was gorgeous, and I wished we could spend it outside.

"You say that every cycle." Gunnar traced a small circle inside my palm with his thumb. My insides fluttered like a swarm of dizzy bumblebees in an untapped lavender field. That god knew how to get to me.

"Mmm… well, I set the oven for a five-hour cook. If this thing goes long, we're looking at a seriously dried out dinner." The bumblebees slowed, probably at the thought of a ruined roast.

"If it goes long, I will barbeque salmon," Ull offered. His mood was considerably lighter now that the Great Hall was in our sights. "We have some from our last fishing trip, right?"

Gunnar nodded. "About twenty pounds, in the storage freezer, mate."

"Great. The two of you can cook if Odin dries out my dinner."

"You going to be okay if Odin makes you Tactical Advisor again?" Gunnar nudged me with his shoulder.

"What do you think?" These meetings had become the bane of my immortal existence. Every five years, Odin handed out jobs for that cycle. And I never got my top choice.

"Listen, Inga—" Ull began.

I cut him off. "You and Gunnar get the jobs you want every cycle. *Every cycle.* And I'm happy for you guys, I really am. You're the best assassins we have. I just want the chance to fight with you."

"I do not fight anymore," Ull offered.

"No, but that was your decision. You spent ten cycles with Gunnar on the Elite Team before you transferred out. You chose to become God of Winter – just like you chose to leave the assassins." My hair bounced across my shoulders as I shook my head. "I'd be lying if I said I wasn't jealous."

"If they let goddesses on the Elite Team, you know you'd be Odin's first choice," Gunnar said. "Well, except for *her.*"

"He could let me be a Valkyrie," I suggested.

"Inga," Ull sighed.

"Why not? I could do it." Valkyries got to harvest mortal soldiers for Odin's collection. The top Valkyries got to train the dead humans to fight for Asgard at Ragnarok. *Such* a sweet deal.

"Sorry. You know how I feel about that." Gunnar dropped my hand.

"Great Odin, still?" I turned to face him. "Gunnar, you *have* to let it go."

"Nope. I'm not going to risk losing you again. I talked to Odin last week. No Valkyries. Sorry."

"Ull." I turned the full force of my blue eyes on him.

"Sorry. I agree with Gunnar on this one. I do not want to lose the closest thing I have to a sister."

The two of them were so overprotective; I could thank the stupid giants for that. If they hadn't kidnapped me forever ago, I could have been fighting alongside my husband instead of sitting in the training room, sketching out battle plans like some fragile ballet mistress. It was excruciating to hand over my carefully orchestrated moves to a group of meatheads who didn't appreciate being taught by a girl. I probably didn't help myself out by leveling the ones who sounded off.

"Fine," I sighed. This was a battle I would never win. Both of my boys were stubborn as an ox.

"It will be all right." Ull gave me the smile every other goddess in Asgard swooned over. Straight teeth, pale pink lips, square jaw... it had zero effect on me.

"Whatever. Let's just go."

We jogged the rest of the way. Ull pointed to three empty seats in the back. We settled in while Odin worked his way down his roster.

"Skadi Snorenson," Odin called from the front of the hall. *The Chosen One* herself clomped toward Odin, waggling her fingers at Ull as she passed our row. *Blech.* "For excellence in combat and service to the realm, you have been reassigned Warrior of Asgard."

Gunnar twirled his finger at his temple and crossed his eyes at me. He leaned so his mouth was against my ear. "She'd be *dritt* at her job if you weren't training her."

I squeezed his thigh. *"Jeg elsker deg."*

"Ditto, doll."

"Bjorn Fiskerdag," Odin continued, as Skadi filed out of the room.

"How much longer is this going to take?" I whispered.

"Knowing Odin, probably two hours." Gunnar rolled his impish green eyes with a wink. If I wasn't so frustrated, they would have been a beautiful distraction.

I murmured, "Hurry it up, for the love of—"

"Big plans?"

"I was hoping somebody might want to take me on a moonlit stroll after dinner." I nudged Gunnar. "You, me, a blanket, and a basket of my freshly baked pastries..."

"Count me in," Ull whispered. "I saw those scones on the counter this morning – wondered what they were for."

Gunnar and I exchanged a glance. Ull had been making himself the third wheel a lot more often lately. He was lonely – plain and simple. Unfortunately, he was also too stubborn to date.

Finally, Odin dismissed Anders. Only Gunnar, Ull and I were left. We sat, backs straight and hands folded in our laps, waiting for the All Father to finish marking his scroll. When he did, Ull nodded.

"Took you long enough, Grandfather."

"Ah, my Terrific *Tre*." Odin's remaining eye crinkled in a smile. He'd lost the other one so long ago, nobody remembered what he'd looked like without the eye patch.

"I presume we shall continue in our posts." Ull stood to leave.

I could never have been that cavalier – the Head of Asgard made me kind of nervous.

"Not quite – sit, son." Odin climbed down from his golden throne and walked our way. Gunnar raised an eyebrow; this was different.

"I do not know if you have heard the rumors." Odin sat across from us in a wooden chair.

Of course we'd heard the rumors. They were all anyone could talk about anymore. Dark factions were allegedly moving to strike Asgard, some kind of a preemptive Ragnarok attack. Travel between the realms had been banned for over a week.

"Does this have anything to do with the Valkyries running the humans through new fight sequences?" Gunnar sounded guarded.

Odin grimaced. "My sources in Alfheim tell me their dark brothers intend to attack soon."

"Svartalfheim? Why don't the light elves stop them?"

Odin shook his head. "You know they have no control over the dark elves."

"So what does this mean?" Ull's eyes narrowed.

"It means that things are changing in Asgard. And I shall need the three of you to change as well."

Oh here it comes, here it comes. Inga Jensson Andersson, I hereby appoint you Head Valkyrie. Junior Valkyrie. Any Valkyrie.

"We will always serve Asgard." Ull's sense of duty had nothing on the overwhelming joy I felt. I was finally going to get to do what I was really good at. And Gunnar couldn't say anything to stop it because the realm *needed* me.

Please, please, please. Please.

"I am glad to hear you say that, Ull. Gunnar, you shall continue to serve as a warrior. We need your leadership, now, more than ever."

"Happy to do my part." Gunnar bowed his head with a smirk. I stopped just short of rolling my eyes. He'd earned the right to be cocky... that was what made him so freaking sexy.

"Inga," Odin continued. I pressed down on my thighs to stop my legs from bouncing. "I shall require that you exercise your gift for analyzing attack patterns to develop the most effective counter moves for the dark elves."

"You need me to fight the dark elves? Hand to hand?" I asked hopefully.

"No, I need you to analyze their movements over the past millennium. Determine their methodology and systematize a counter attack to debilitate them."

My shoulders dropped. Bloody Helheim. The end of the cosmos was upon us, and I *still* had to be an advisor?

"Yes, Odin." I blinked back tears.

Gunnar rubbed my back with the tips of his fingers. "Sorry."

I shrugged in reply.

"And Ull, I shall need to shift your duties as well."

"Grandfather." Ull's voice had an edge.

Odin held up his hand. "I understand, but you must protect your realm. You know this."

"What are you asking of me?"

Odin held Ull's gaze. "For the time being, and remember this is only until the threat from Svartalfheim has been eliminated…"

"Yes?"

"You shall set aside your post as God of Winter and pick up the duties of God of War."

Oh, no. This was not going to be pretty.

"That is Tyr's job." Ull growled.

"He is… otherwise occupied."

"Grandfather, I cannot accept. We have discussed this." Ull kept his voice steady but his jaw twitched. That wasn't a good sign.

"And I have respected your feelings in the past. But the well-being of Asgard is at stake, and I need my strongest warrior overseeing the battle."

"I would never turn my back on my realm. I will fight. But you cannot ask me to take that title." The twitch in Ull's jaw kept rhythm with his clenched fist. He was seriously displeased with this turn of events.

"I am not asking." Odin stood. "You shall assume the post God of War, effective immediately. Meet me in my chambers at sunrise to discuss our strategy." With that, Odin swept from the Great Hall, his golden robes billowing behind him.

This was so not good.

I caught Gunnar's look and closed my eyes. We wound our fingers together, and waited for the tirade to begin.

It only took Ull ten minutes to work through his anger. First came the shouting; then a few chairs were thrown, and finally, a flag was ripped from the rafters. Gunnar and I had seen it hundreds of times before. Ull's temper was rivaled only by his stubbornness, and he'd made it more than clear to Odin that his assassin days were behind him.

"Sorry, mate," Gunnar offered when Ull sat down.

"I will not do it," Ull muttered, head in hands.

"You have to," I whispered. "It's a command."

Ull raked his fingers through his hair and slumped back in the chair. "I can fight. I cannot oversee the attacks."

"You're going to have to collect the families, aren't you?" Gunnar asked.

Ull nodded. It was the oldest trick in the battle book. Asgard was notorious for going after the families of infidels and holding them hostage, to force our enemies to back down. It was lousy, underhanded and cruel – but Odin always said, all's fair in war. And the Father of All Things knows best… even when he was being completely and totally heartless.

"I'm so sorry," I said.

"Me too." Gunnar clapped Ull on the back.

We sat in the Great Hall until the sun started to set. My roast would be ruined, but I didn't care. None of us had the energy to head home. Who knew what the morning would bring?

As it turned out it, the morning was the least of our concerns. Nightfall was what we needed to worry about.

CHAPTER 2

W E'D **BARELY MADE IT** home when the sirens started blaring. I shot Gunnar an uneasy look as we raced to our bedroom, throwing dress robes on the floor, and suiting up in black combat gear. I grabbed my rapier and dagger from the hall closet and tossed Gunnar his crossbow. By the time we got back to the front door, Ull was already in his fatigues, battle sword in hand.

"Go," Ull commanded. We obeyed. Despite his feelings on the subject, he was the best fighter among us.

We ran through the night, down the dark meadow and past the pond. The Great Hall filled as we entered, gods and goddesses moving into ranks. Ull took his place at the head of the hall alongside Thor. Together, they were a peculiar pair – one a battle-scarred redhead who looked like the stereotypical Midgardian Viking; the other a fierce blond assassin who looked like he might moonlight as a movie star. But they shared the same set jaw, the same intense look, and emitted the same waves of fury. Whatever was going down, it was serious. Gunnar and I stood in front of Ull and waited for our orders.

"Asgardians," Odin's somber tone rose through the

frenzy. "Svartalfheim has attacked the Bifrost. Dark Elves overtook Heimdall and are crossing the bridge. I believe their goal is simple destruction, but we must protect the Unknowables nonetheless. Anders, your team is to guard the War Cabinet. Bjorn, ensure your men protect the Treasure Room. Dagnir, oversee the Sanctimony. And Magni, patrol the residential areas. The rest of you, follow Thor to the Bifrost."

My brain clicked into fight mode, and I clenched my rapier in my left hand. I barely noticed Gunnar's tug on my jacket as he pulled me to the wall.

"Inga," he whispered. "Please be careful."

"You too, baby." I smiled. I knew he was worried, but I couldn't contain my elation. I hadn't seen a real fight in a century. Anticipation thrummed in my veins.

"I mean it. You are my life, and if anything happened to you—"

I cut him off before he could get too sentimental. "Zip it, Andersson." I kissed him gently, melting against his soft lips. "Save it for the after party back home." He raised an eyebrow and I curled up against him for the briefest of moments before we righted ourselves and fell back into rank. Ull moved in to my side and relayed Thor's orders.

"The two of you are to stay with me. For some reason Thor thinks I am a target, and he wants Gunnar at my flank. Inga, you are free to follow Skadi's group to rescue Heimdall. But, knowing how you feel about her, I asked for your assistance as well. Is that all right?"

"Thanks, Ull." Doing anything at Skadi's command would be suicide. She made stupid mistakes trying to prove she was tough enough for a god's job, and I had no intention of getting myself killed because of her ego.

"Now if anything happens, Gunnar, we protect Inga first. Get her to safety."

"Hey," I protested. "I can take care of myself."

"I know you can." Ull chuckled. "Or I would send you back to the house right now."

"I wouldn't go." I put my hands on my hips. If Ull thought he could keep me away from this fight, he had another thing coming.

"Yes, you would. No matter. Come." He jogged into the darkness, away from the troupe filing steadfastly behind Thor. His muscular form ran lithely toward the trees, then disappeared. That was weird – protocol dictated we stay with the others. A three-person hunting party would be easy for an enemy to pick off.

Ull knew something he wasn't telling us.

Gunnar raised an eyebrow and shrugged. I shifted my weapons to my left hand as we jogged into the woods after Ull. It'd been a long time since I'd been in the Dark Forest, and it still gave me chills. Asymmetrical trees cast shadows across uneven footpaths and the eerie silence confirmed that all the animals had fled. Someone – or something – was in here.

"Ull," Gunnar began. Ull held up a hand, and Gunnar fell silent. We followed him deeper into the forest, for Odin knows how long, until we heard a low grumbling. Dropping behind a quintet of boulders, we held our breaths, listening to the foreign voices coming from the clearing. I'd taken Svartish in secondary school, but it'd been a while since I'd tried to conjugate the verbs. *Enter the chamber; decapitate Odin; end the bloodline...* oh Ymir. The dark elves were going after Odin. The next in the bloodline was Thor. And after that was...

"Get out of here. Now!" Gunnar shoved Ull. The three of us took off at an even sprint, two massive killers shepherding me through the thick wood. Thor was right – Ull was a target. He was the last of the royal bloodline, even if it was through marriage. If the royal bloodline was eliminated, it could take a year to go through the electoral process to select a new king. Asgard would be leaderless and totally suscep-tible to attacks. It would be the perfect time to incite Ragnarok.

I ran like my life depended on it. In all likelihood, it prob-ably did. The dark elves might keep me as a hostage, but that wasn't how I planned to spend the rest of my days. My arms pumped as I willed myself through the forest. Keeping pace with Gunnar and Ull was easy enough, but without warning a tree fell across the river, stopping us all.

A voice broke through the darkness, speaking in English. "Going somewhere?"

I whipped around, my back against Gunnar's in a defen-sive position. I held my rapier at eye level, keeping my dagger at my hip. The muscles in Gunnar's back tensed against mine as I felt him flex his crossbow. Without having to look, I knew his chin was down, his knees were bent, and his arms were raised to pull the trigger. He was ready to fight.

"Show yourself," Ull commanded, now two feet ahead of me. His shoulder blades were pulled back and his elbows were slightly bent. A lock of blond hair ruffled in the breeze, but other than that he didn't move; he'd taken up a protective stance.

"Ah, but what would be the fun in that? I would much prefer you meet my friend." A muffled voice erupted in laughter from somewhere in the shadows and another tree fell across the river. The tree rose, then fell again, closer to us. My knees buckled, and for the first time I felt the tiniest bit of fear. That wasn't a tree at all. It was...

"A giant," Gunnar whispered, pressing his back closer to mine. No doubt he was thinking about what happened the last time a giant breached Asgard. I'd been kidnapped; a half dozen warriors died saving me. It ended well enough, with Gunnar charging to my rescue and realizing I was *the one* for him and all. But, it hadn't exactly been a pleasure cruise for me. Or for my saviors.

"It's all right. I've got this." I did. Of the three of us, I'd been the only one to spend any goodly amount of time with a giant. I knew they had a weakness for pretty girls. And I knew they got distracted by shiny things. I stepped into the creature's sightline and tossed my white-blonde hair behind my shoulder.

"You want me?" I raised my chin to shout into the sky. It was generally understood that giants were somewhat hard of hearing.

"What are you thinking? Stop that!" Ull hissed.

"I know what I'm doing." I shushed him. Gunnar gave me a nod. "Down here, you want me?"

The giant looked around until his eyes focused. Slowly, he bent down with a hand outstretched. I stood very still.

"That's it," I called up. "Come and get me."

From the corner of my eye I saw a spiky-haired warrior aim his bow.

"Now," I screamed.

Gunnar let the arrow fly, catching the giant in the eyeball. The beast roared and stumbled backwards, yanking the object free.

"Again, Gunnar!"

My avenging assassin leapt from the trees. He soared through the air, arms cocked with his crossbow held at eye level. When his body was parallel with the giant's waist, he let four arrows fly in succession. They struck the monster's chest with a wet splice, blood dripping from the points of impact in a thick stream. The giant tripped over a fallen tree and fell into the stream, cracking his skull on a sharp boulder.

"One down." Gunnar lifted one corner of his mouth in a grin. But there wasn't time to celebrate. A unit of dark elves quickly filed out of the forest, their swords glinting in the filtered light. Ull raised his blade to draw their attention.

"Get Inga out of here," Ull instructed.

Gunnar pushed me into the trees. Ull stood his ground, swinging his sword at the onslaught of dark elves. They weren't the brightest beams in the Bifrost, and although they outnumbered us by twenty, they hadn't undergone the centuries of training we had.

"Stay here. Please." Gunnar cupped my cheeks with warm palms.

My hand twitched around my weapons. "I can't."

"I know." He sighed. "But I had to try."

We ran back to Ull's side and took up arms.

"I told you to get Inga to safety." Ull grunted as he struck an elf between the shoulders.

"You know she doesn't listen to me."

"I'm not sitting this out." I swung my rapier over my head and plunged it into an oncoming sternum. I tossed my hair over my shoulder as I withdrew my blade. "Do you know me at all?"

"I know you all right." Ull shook his head as he raised thick arms and brought them down at a ninety-degree angle, decapitating one of Svartalfheim's finest. Blood shot everywhere. "Stubborn... pigheaded... unbelievably frus- trating..."

"Asgardian beauty queen, award winning baker... patience of a saint to put up with you," I countered as I fought off the next attacker.

"Stop it you two," Gunnar groaned. He delivered a series of jabs to his opponent's face. "You're distracting me. Oh, enough of this hand to hand *dritt*. We're wasting time." He swung his crossbow around and started to fire. He quickly eliminated ten of the intruders with his arrows. I took down two more.

It was incredible.

Years of frustration at not being taken seriously by the Asgardian aristocracy were wiped clean with each thrust and parry. These elves were flat out stupid to try and mess with

Ull. Nobody was going to come after my family and get away with it.

With only three to go, we closed ranks and moved in. The survivors were the strongest fighters, and for the first time, I began to fatigue. I pocketed my dagger, using both hands to exert the full force of the rapier on my attacker. He was strong, and I was exhausted. He backed me a good twenty feet from my partners, down the river. I fought back, but he outmaneuvered me. This guy was seriously quick for a dark elf. They were supposed to be slow in movement and thought. But this one was too fast for me to keep up. He had the long legs and slender build residents of Svartalfheim were known for, but something about his face was off. Instead of being angular and sallow, it was rounder, with a slightly bluish tint. If I didn't know it was impossible, I would have thought he was some kind of hybrid.

"Well, Inga," my attacker seethed. It was the voice I'd heard from the shadows. "It seems you're quite literally up a creek. Who will save you now?"

"How do you know my name?" I jabbed at his torso and he expertly sidestepped my move.

"Silly girl." He knocked my sword aside and in one swift move had me suspended by my hair. "I know everything." He ripped the dagger out of my pocket and held it against my throat.

In the nanosecond it took me to register what was happening, I sought out Gunnar. The boys were locked in battle with two enormous residents of Svartalfheim. Gunnar threw a punch at his opponent, then sent two arrows through the perp's chest before his victim hit the ground. Man down.

Gunnar looked up and saw me dangling from a dark elf's fist. His anguished cry ripped through the woods. "No!"

It was equal parts adorable and insulting. I might have

been minus a rapier, with my own dagger jammed against my throat, but this was nothing I couldn't handle.

"I've got this," I muttered for the second time that day. And with strength that most titled gods would have envied, I ripped my rival's hand from my neck. I tucked my knees to my chest and somersaulted out of the surprised elf's grasp, landing on my feet. I reached into the river and pulled out a rock. It was too smooth to cut elf skin, but I lobbed it at his head anyway. The smashing of bones produced a sickening crunch. He reached up to catch the blood oozing from his nose.

Before he could retaliate, I followed up with a graceful roundhouse to his jaw. The slap of my boot on his flesh echoed all the way up the river.

"Atta girl!" Gunnar's voice pinged with pride. "You need me?"

"No, baby." My palm closed around a suitably sharp stone as I ducked just in time to avoid a fist to my face. "Go help Ull." I wedged the crude weapon between my middle and ring fingers.

"Done," Gunnar called out, apparently satisfied that I did, indeed, have this fight under control.

Stone in place, I landed a left hook on my challenger's cheek. His face was going to be seriously bruised at the end of this – if he survived. I wasn't feeling terribly benevolent. The jerk had taken my best dagger.

"Oh, Inga." The elf seethed before landing a fist to my stomach. It knocked the wind out of me, and I doubled over.

"Go to Helheim." I took a deep breath and let loose with a kick sequence I'd been preparing to teach my unit that week. Left roundhouse, right hook, hitch kick. He stumbled back. Front kick to his chest. He stumbled again. Side kick, side kick, one more hitch. To finish him off, I planted a jab to his face, piercing him between the eyes with the sharp end of the rock.

He went down hard, hitting his skull on one of the boulders resting in the river. His eyes locked on mine, widening just a fraction before I delivered a kick to his head.

"That's for taking my dagger." I bent and ripped my beloved blade from his hand. Some fighter he was; he hadn't even scratched me with it.

I kicked him in the torso, and he bent in half, clutching his freshly fractured sternum. "And that's for getting my sword wet." I stood over him for a good minute but he didn't move. Satisfied that he wasn't going anywhere, I scoured the water until I found my rapier. I picked it up and slowly made my way back to the dark elf writhing in the river.

"Gunnar?" I called upstream. "What's the verdict?"

"No survivors," he shouted back.

"Fair enough." I raised my sword and held my breath, feeling the impact of my rapier piercing the elf's flesh. It was combat 101 – there was no way to survive a strike to the heart.

When I was sure the elf wouldn't get up again, I cleaned the blood off my sword in the river. Then, I dried the blade on the edge of my shirt and made my way back to Ull and Gunnar.

"Nice work, boys." I held up my palm, and Ull slapped me a high five, a grin lighting up his angular face. He had drops of sweat lining his forehead, and a lock of dirt-caked blond hair fell over one twinkling eye. For a guy retired from the Elite Team, he sure seemed to enjoy a good fight.

Gunnar strapped his bow around his back so his hands were free. "You too, doll." He wrapped one arm around my waist and leaned me back, his face an inch from mine. A devilish smile played on his lips as he breathed into my ear. "For a minute there you had me worried, Andersson."

"Just keeping you on your toes." He smelled so delicious – like sweat mixed with metal, topped with just the tiniest dash of blood. I turned my face into his neck, brushing my lips against the drops lingering at his collarbone.

"I expect nothing less." Gunnar made a fist in my hair. In one rough movement, he pulled my head up. His emerald eyes sparked with the charge of adrenaline and fear and relief we always got after a fight. The arm around my waist tightened as he pulled my hips into his. Then he brought his face down, crushing my mouth in a hot rush. His tongue probed my lips until they gave way. He moved against me in a languorous dance, warm and sweet. The unhurried movements of his mouth were the antithesis to the frantic pull of his hands. They tugged at my shirt with feverish need, grabbing at the fabric until it rode up my torso. When my skin was exposed, Gunnar slid the hand that wasn't gripping my hair across my stomach. He palmed my abdomen, his thumb stroking the taut surface while his fingers dug against my flesh. I let out an unwitting sigh as he massaged the muscles that were still tense from battle. They loosened stroke by stroke, and I slowly melted into him.

"*Faen*, Inga. You're hot when you kill things." Gunnar cupped my behind with one hand and hiked me onto his hip. *Gods, that felt amazing.* I wrapped my legs around his waist and kissed him frenetically as he slammed our bodies against a tree. The bark felt rough against my back, a sharp contrast to the gentle caress of Gunnar's tongue at my neck. I threw my head back as he licked a trail from my jaw to my chest. When he got to the neckline of my shirt he swore. "*Helvetes* shirt."

Gunnar shoved his knee between my legs, pinning me against the tree so he could free his hands. He raked my flesh with his teeth, biting at the curve of my neck just hard enough to make me shiver. He brought both hands to the bottom of my shirt, but as he moved to rip it over my head, Ull cleared his throat.

"I am still here." I could practically hear him rolling his eyes.

"So?" Gunnar retorted, still tugging at my shirt. "Go away."

"We need to check on Thor's team." Ull Myhr, always the voice of reason. Also the consummate party pooper.

A slow breath escaped my lips. Lives were on the line. My hormones could wait… for a few hours, tops. "They could probably use the extra fighters," I admitted.

"You are such a buzz kill, you know that?" Gunnar glared at Ull. He put his hands around my waist and lowered me to the ground. While I straightened the front of my shirt, Gunnar brushed the bark off my back.

"Somebody has to keep things in check around here." Ull crossed his arms.

"Look, just because you're not getting any doesn't mean you have to spoil it for the rest of us." Gunnar ran a hand through his hair. The dimple in his cheek softened his words.

"At least I can control myself," Ull shook his head, "Can you say the same?"

"Oh, Gunnar has *exceptional* control." I ran my fingers through my husband's hair, fluffing the tips so they stood up in telltale disarray. "Don't you, babe?"

"You know it." Gunnar shot me my favorite naughty grin as Ull stomped up the river. He adjusted the settings on his crossbow as we traversed out of the forest, then took my hand in his. "We've got to get you a girlfriend, mate."

"Would not matter," Ull kept a steady pace, "Unlike some of you, I do not let hormones interfere with my duties."

"We were planning to go back to the battlefield," I reasoned. "We were just catching our breath for, like, one minute. One minute wouldn't have hurt anyone."

"It'd have taken more than one minute," Gunnar whispered in my ear. My cheeks grew warm.

Ull ignored us as we walked into the clearing. "Huh. Well, I suppose you were right. We were not needed here."

The sun was starting to rise over the meadow, setting an eerie glow over the scene. Thor's party had done just fine without us. Piles of dark elves lay across the battlefield, their remnants smoldering in heaps. My nose wrinkled. Asgard had won this fight. And from the stench of the carcasses, I knew Svartalfheim had given up impressive numbers.

CHAPTER 3

THE NEXT AFTERNOON, I stood in Odin's office, making the most important argument of my life.

"I single-handedly took down that dark elf, not to mention the other twenty or so the three of us took out together. And at the same time, we uncovered the plot against the bloodline and informed you of the threat so you know to double your guards. Goddesses *can* be invaluable members of the combat team. I want to be a warrior." I finished my case with a small bow and waited for Odin to promote me from the administrative position that would have already bored me to death if not for the whole immortal thing.

"I see. Anything else?" Odin raised the brow over his remaining eye. While I'd been talking, he hadn't so much as shifted in his heavy leather chair. Instead, he'd sat stiller than the statue at the base of the Bifrost, with his heavy silver robes draped over his uncrossed legs and his weathered fingers calmly clasped in front of him. The rest of us embraced civilian wear, but Odin insisted on formal dress, always. And from his robes to his stare, nothing about him gave me the impression that I'd moved him *at all*.

"Well, in the event you aren't swayed by the facts, which we both know you will be, I baked these cookies to change your mind." I set the basket on his desk.

"Gingersnaps. My grandmother's recipe."

"Jens' mother? That is a fine recipe."

"I know." I crossed my ankles and waited for the news I'd spent an eternity hoping to hear. Odin picked up a cookie and took a bite.

"Well done. These are wonderful." He wiped the crumbs from his mouth with the napkin I handed him.

"Thanks. So how about it? When can I start?"

"When can you start what?" Odin reached for a second cookie, but I intercepted his hand.

"When can I start training as a warrior?"

"Oh, Inga," Odin pushed past my hand and picked up another cookie, "I cannot let you do that."

"Why? I proved I'm every bit as good in battle as Skadi, and you let her fight."

"Skadi's father is not my most trusted advisor."

"So, this is about my father?" I blinked back angry tears. "He can't run my life forever."

"He is not running your life." Odin's voice was soft. "He runs mine. And I need him to continue doing so. Jens would never recover if anything were to happen to you, and I do not know where I would find another advisor with such an understanding of our people."

"Fabulous." I closed my eyes. "I can't be a warrior because you don't want to upset my dad?"

"I know it seems unfair—"

"It is unfair! Nothing bad would happen to me if you let me fight. I would be fine. Absolutely fine, just like I always am. I'm the best swordsman this realm's ever seen."

Odin set the cookie down. "I know you are."

"No you don't. If you did, you'd want me fighting for you. Helheim, you'd want me to be your personal bodyguard." My outburst was out of character; I was usually much more reserved around Odin.

"I would love to have you fight for me. I know you are a better fighter than Skadi."

"Really?" I crossed my arms.

"Yes. You are even tempered and calm where she is hot headed and insecure. She is going to get herself killed in her effort to prove her worth."

"I've been saying that for eons," I muttered.

"You are much too valuable to me to risk your life in battle. I have scores of Asgardians who can fight for me, but only two who look after my grandson."

"You let Gunnar fight."

"I do." Odin nodded. "And that is why I cannot let you."

"But Odin—"

"Enough. My answer is no. Thank you for your service, both against the dark elves and in obtaining the information that saved my life."

"So that's it? Just no?"

"Just no." Odin held my gaze.

"But what if—"

"There is nothing more to say on the matter. Please see yourself out." Odin reached for some correspondence and began to read. When I didn't move, he glanced up. "Good day, Inga."

I stood, my anger bubbling dangerously close to the surface. "Good day, Odin." And before I could think about what I was doing, I snatched the basket of cookies from his desk and stormed out of his office.

"Your stupid, closed minded, backwards grandfather!" I burst through the front door of the house, ready to rip into my friend for his family's offense. Gunnar was debriefing the

Elite Team after the dark elf attacks, so I could let loose on Ull without anyone jumping in. "He *still* won't let me fight, after everything I did for him! It's so—"

I broke off. Ull was sitting at the kitchen table, in his favorite grey sweatpants and an Academy tank top. He must have just taken a shower because he smelled like the cedar-scented shampoo I'd picked up for him last week. His arms were straight out in front of him, hands clasping a mug, and his cheek rested on the tabletop. Even his hair was dejected, flopping listlessly on the wood beneath his face. If he'd been a sculpture, the artist would have named him, *Morose*.

"Great Asgard, Ull, what's wrong?"

"He is fixated on this God of War nonsense." Ull didn't raise his head.

"Odin?" I asked.

"One and the same," he confirmed.

"Jeez, why won't he just *listen* to us?" I threw the basket of gingersnaps in the garbage and opened the door to the pantry. "It's not like we don't know what we're talking about. I'd make an exceptional warrior, and you'd make a terrible God of War. You're way too sensitive. Sorry." I grabbed baking powder, salt, flour, and sugar, and stomped back into the kitchen, slamming the pantry door so hard the glass shook.

"No, you are right. I would make a terrible God of War. The last thing I want to do is devote eternity to orchestrating destruction."

"Well, the only thing I want to do is fight. I'm so sick of sitting behind a desk, sketching out choreography for everyone else to use but me." I opened the door of our stainless steel refrigerator and pulled out butter, milk and Mexican vanilla. It was a bear to convince Heimdall to open the Bifrost so I could go grocery shopping, but the Mexican variety was vastly superior to the Asgardian bean. I threw the wet ingredients into the bowl of my standing mixer and turned it on.

"Fighting is not all it is cracked up to be, Inga." Ull still hadn't looked up.

"You want me to heat up that tea?" I gestured to his full cup.

"Please."

I reheated his tea and crossed to the freezer where I pulled out a bar of semi-sweet chocolate. I grabbed a cutting board, and brought my new meat cleaver to the table.

"What are you making?" Ull asked.

"Chocolate chip cookies." I set to work chopping.

"Pretty serious knife for cutting chocolate." Ull finally looked up.

"Yeah, well, I'm in a serious kind of mood."

"Odin is not going to let you fight. I am sorry, but the sooner you accept *what is,* the faster you can move on." He took a drink, the bags under his large eyes betraying his exhaustion.

"Oh, really? And how's accepting *what is* working out for you, Mr. God of War- elect?" I carried the cutting board to my mixer and scraped the chocolate pieces into the batter.

"Terribly." Ull sighed.

"So what are you going to do?" I doubted this would be a real problem. Ull was Odin's favorite; he pretty much got everything he wanted. Whatever bee had flown up Odin's bonnet this week had him seriously out of sorts.

Ull shook his head. "Continue to refuse, I suppose. What else can I do?"

"Well… it depends. Odin's obviously in a foul mood, right? The whole 'attack on the bloodline' thing has him all wound up. He's worrying about Ragnarok."

"I would say so." Ull took another drink.

"So." I shrugged. "Let's get out of here."

"Pardon?"

"Get out of here. Take a vacation. It's not like he needs us around – he's doubled his guard after the attacks. And we haven't gotten away in forever. We need the break."

My motives weren't entirely selfish. Yes, I was beyond frustrated with Odin, and it would serve him right if his top fight choreographer took some time off. But I had another reason for wanting to take Ull away from Asgard. A very pretty reason with a lovely name. *Kristia Tostenson.*

"Where do you want to go?" Ull looked interested. That was a good sign.

"Well, we haven't been to Earth in a while. Remember how much fun we always have playing human at their universities? And I only need to earn one more degree to bring my total up to an even twenty." Or was it thirty? I lost count after the whole Ivy League tour.

"You want to go to Midgard and pretend to be college students. Again."

I grinned. "Just like old times." It was a fun break from our regular jobs, plus it was hysterical to watch the human girls react to Ull. A shocking number of them actually went into giggling fits when he spoke to them. It was slightly less amusing when they giggled at Gunnar, but his wedding band managed to deflect a few of the hormonal co-eds. The rest could deal with me.

"Midgard might be nice," Ull mused. "But Odin would never let us take off for four years with everything that is going on. The most we could ask for is two, tops."

"Then we get graduate degrees. Or do the undergrad thing and doctor up some transfer papers from one of those Scandinavian universities so we go in as juniors. If you're up for the trip, I'll deal with the logistics."

"*Hei hei.*" I heard Gunnar's deep voice before I saw him. He came into the kitchen wearing his standard black cargoes and a tank top that showcased the results of his twice-daily workouts. He dropped his duffle bag at the door and made a beeline for me. "There's my girl." He put both hands on my hips and pulled me into him.

"Hey, babe." I smiled. "I missed you." Gunnar ran his nose along my ear and nipped at the lobe. My eyes rolled back as he kissed his way down my jaw, along my neck, and back up to my mouth. He really was an amazing kisser.

"We were just talking about a vacation," Ull said pointedly. "Yes, still here."

"Sorry, Ull. Gunnar, sit." I drew back and kissed Gunnar's cheek just as the timer beeped. I grabbed my oven mitts and removed the tray. Crossing to the cabinet, I pulled out three glasses and filled them with milk, then brought the cookies to the table. The boys loved this recipe.

"So where are we going on this vacation?" Gunnar asked through a mouthful of melting chocolate.

"Midgard."

"Oh, Midgard. Fun. Hey, isn't the chick from Elsker's prophecy supposed to be there now? Are we going to track her down? Ouch! Why'd you kick me, Inga?" Gunnar looked genuinely surprised.

So did Ull. Eighteen years ago, our favorite seer, Elsker, predicted Ull's ideal mate would show up at Cardiff University on Midgard. Every time Ull went into one of his dark moods, I counted down the number of days until her arrival. How my friend could think I'd forgotten about this was beyond me.

"Is that what this is about?" Ull's brow furrowed. He was probably adding up years in his head. "Oh, Inga. No. I do not want to meet the human."

"Just hear me out," I pleaded. "All you've ever wanted is to have your own family. Elsker said your soul mate would be in Wales next year. You go, you meet her, you fall in love, you have baby gods… everybody wins."

"Forget it. Elsker was wrong. I do not have a soul mate. Especially not a human one."

Ugh, I hated the sound of grinding teeth. For a formidable killer, Ull could do self-pity like no-one else.

"No, I won't forget it. Asgard sucks right now. I'm stuck behind a desk, and you're about to be God of Doom and Gloom. Why can't we go to Cardiff, earn a couple more degrees, maybe get you a girlfriend?"

"That is too much pressure." Ull stared into his teacup.

"Just think about it, okay, mate? We all need the vacation. And you don't have to talk to the girl," Gunnar urged. He always had my back.

"I will think about it," Ull agreed. "That is *all* I will do."

I grinned at Gunnar. It was all the opening I needed.

CARDIFF WAS LOVELY. We rented a two-bedroom house off campus and I did a bang up job of decorating. Between twenty-four hour home furniture delivery and the miracle of internet shopping, Midgard had gotten so much more civilized since our last visit.

But months went by, and the human didn't show up. Despite Ull's protests to the contrary, I knew he was disappointed. We'd come all this way hoping to get a glimpse of the alleged love of his existence, and she was nowhere to be found.

It was obvious Ull was at his wit's end when I caught him dodging a crowd of giggling co-eds.

"Come on." I pulled my friend away from the hormonal horde. "I have something to show you."

"What?" Ull dragged his feet.

"Stop it. I just got you those shoes." Ull was going to scuff the exquisite Italian lace-ups I'd picked up on the internet. Shopping on Midgard in the twenty-first century was brilliant.

"They're *shoes*, Inga."

"They are perfection in leather," I corrected. "And just walk normally. You're going to like what I have to show you."

"Fine." Ull followed me into the administration building.

"Good morning Inga," called the receptionist. I'd been buttering her up all week.

"Happy Friday, Bianca." I smiled. "May I please see that form you showed me?"

"You know I'm not supposed to release confidential information." The receptionist glanced over her shoulder, fingering her glossy brown locks. "But, it really is the least I can do after those amazing cookies you brought by yesterday."

"It was nothing. Here's the recipe." I produced a piece of paper, and the girl's eyes lit up. Humans were so cute.

"Oh, thank you! I'm going to make these for my boyfriend this weekend!"

"He'll love them," I promised.

"I hope so." She crossed to the counter with a piece of paper. "I'll just give you a moment with this. If anyone asks—"

"I know. I found it on the floor and brought it to the counter without looking at it." I winked as she scurried off.

"An enrollment form. Great Inga. How does this affect me at all?" Ull checked his watch.

"Well… have you looked at the form?"

Ull sighed and glanced at the paper. "New student paperwork. So what?"

His impatience was beyond frustrating. Was he really that dense? "Ull. Read. The. Form."

With an incredibly inappropriate eye roll, he did.

What happened next was adorable.

"Come on, doll. You have to tell me what he said." Gunnar

pulled the drapes across the doors that led from our bedroom to the tiny garden. Night fell later as the summer went on, and it was nearly eleven by the time we were done summarizing training sequences, approving attack plans, finishing our homework, and doing the dishes.

"I can't." I put my toothbrush down. "It would embarrass him."

"Don't hold out on me, Andersson. I have ways of making you talk." Gunnar crossed to the bed and turned down the sheets. He patted the downy white comforter with a look that made my insides glow. "Get over here."

My hair whipped back and forth. "No way. That's not playing fair."

"Who said I play fair?" Gunnar's dimple popped. He strolled to my side, scooped me up in his arms, and carried me to the bed. His biceps flexed with each step, hard muscle pressing against my silky robe. I stroked the stubble of his jaw as we moved, feeling the coarse fibers beneath my fingertips. *Gods, I loved it when he forgot to shave.* With four long strides, we reached the bed. Gunanr laid me on the Egyptian cotton sheets and positioned himself with one knee on each side of my hips. "Now, cough up the intel, woman."

"Forget it." I tried to shove him away, laughing. But Gunnar was insistent.

"This could be the best Ull Myhr story ever. And as my wife, your property is my property. Including your epic, mortifying Myhr experiences. If you won't cough it up, I can resort to a more creative tactic." He ran both palms along the sides of my ribs with agonizing slowness, firmly pressing the taut muscles beneath. When he got to my chest his eyes glazed over. Gods, he was such a *guy.* The tips of his fingers grazed the outline of the lacy bra beneath my robe. The light sensation brought a rush of blood, and I could feel my skin swell under his touch. I breathed deeply, arching my back just enough to fill Gunnar's hand.

"*Faen*," he swore. He squeezed gently, then ripped my robe open.

"Gunnar!" I squealed.

He ran his fingers along the lace of my bra. "*Dritt*. You had to wear the black one." He lifted his hips and tugged the robe free so I was completely exposed. "With the bloody matching panties," he complained.

"You were saying?"

"I have no *helvetes* idea." He dropped his head, and I gasped. His mouth was hot against my stomach. His lips moved against my abdomen, slowly making their way up to what he dang well knew was my weak spot. When he reached the underwire, I stilled. There was one thing Gunnar Andersson did *extremely* well. Interrogate. And much as I wanted to keep Ull's secret, I wasn't sure how much I wanted to stop this.

"I'm not talking," I reiterated. "No matter what you do to me."

"Oh no?" Gunnar looked up lazily, the proverbial canary eating cat. He wrapped long fingers around my wrists and held my hands together over my head. Then he brought his nose to the top of my bra, running it along the lace. He exhaled softly as he moved, leaving a cool trail in his wake. My body squirmed at the sensation. With his free hand, he pulled at the fabric. He blew gently on the bare skin, then met my eyes with a smirk. "You sure about that?"

At the moment, I wasn't sure of anything. Except that I was very, *very* happy to be exactly where I was.

"I'm not talking," I swore. But the words came on a question, and Gunnar decided he'd won.

"Sure you're not." He lowered his head so his mouth hovered just over my now burning flesh. He let out a breath, and I arched again, willing him to drop his head just an inch lower. I felt him chuckle on top of me; the throaty sound made his torso vibrate. "You have something I want, and I have something you want. How about we work a trade?"

"No," I resolved. But my body said otherwise. I twitched beneath him, twisting against his hold in a pointless effort to make contact.

"No can do, baby. I want intel." He shifted his hips, and a thousand nerve endings sprung to life. That god could do things to me… Gunnar was clearly stronger than I was, in all the ways that mattered.

I tried a different tack. I softly raised my chin as I pushed out my lower lip. My eyes widened, and I blinked slowly, tilting my head to the side.

"*Dritt*, Inga. That's not fair."

"Who said I play fair?" I threw his words back at him.

He let out a growl and released my hands. They flew to his hair as I pulled closer.

"Gunnar," I moaned.

"You going to talk yet?" His tongue moved in slow circles against my neck, bringing me to the edge of crazy. My hands fisted in his hair, and I turned my face to the side to bite the pillow.

"Oh my gods, Gunnar. You're killing me. Can we please just drop it?"

"Drop what?" He murmured, lips brushing my ear.

"Exactly." I sighed. Then, I grabbed his biceps and closed my eyes.

And that's how I kept Ull's secret. Honorable? Probably not. Effective? Definitely. Because Gunnar never knew Ull picked up the admissions form and stood still for so long, I worried someone might walk in on us. When he finally moved, it was to place the paper on the counter with care. His eyes misted over, and he swiped at them so quickly I wasn't sure the tears had actually been there. He stood for a long moment staring at his clasped hands. When he looked up, his face was reverent.

"She's coming in the fall." Ull's voice was so hopeful it nearly broke my heart. He'd been alone for so long. We desperately wanted this for him. For all of us. Gods, I hoped Elsker's prophecy hadn't been wrong – there was no way we could weather the fallout. "Kristia Tostenson." Ull said the human's name on a breath, projecting hundreds of years of solitude into six tense syllables.

Oh, Great Odin. It was on.

See what happens when Inga, Gunnar and Ull meet Kristia in
ELSKER.

Kristia is stunned to discover that her boyfriend, Ull Myhr,
isn't even human. He's a Norse god, forbidden to love and
destined to die in a battle that will destroy Earth. But these
two just might break all the rules — and save the world while
they're at it…

And now, a sneak peek at ELSKER . . .

"KRISTIA!" I HEARD ULL'S voice before I saw him. He burst through the back door of the nightclub and pulled me into a hug. "Are you all right?"

"Yes. Where did you go?" Ull's chest muffled my question.

"I took your assailant outside. Dealt with the problem."

I tried to pull away, but Ull was too strong. "Let go." He did, reluctantly. "I mean where did you go? You just…disappeared."

"I walked outside." Ull shrugged.

"No, you didn't. You had that guy by the neck, and then he said I was asking for it and you just—" I twirled my finger. "Poof. Gone."

"It has been a long night. Wait here," Ull commanded. While I didn't appreciate taking orders, I didn't challenge him. Ull had a brief talk with the bartender, no doubt making sure the perps couldn't cause any more harm, and came back with our coats on his arm. I didn't ask how he had known which jacket was mine.

"Come Kristia, I am taking you home." He strode across the dance floor, still radiating barely-contained fury, as I hastily told my roommates I'd meet them at our flat. Once outside, Ull stopped under a streetlight. Tension rippled from his body, but his eyes were soft; the grey-blue of the sky after a storm. I both adored and hated him all at once.

"How are you feeling?"

"I'm fine. How did you…"

Ull drew another ragged breath. "Right place, right time." He obviously wasn't telling the whole truth.

"That's not what I mean. Are you going to tell me about that whole disappearing act in the club?" Or explain how he and his stepdad had the same names as the gods I'd taken a quiz on this week?

"Not tonight."

"Then goodnight."

"Wait." He seemed at a loss. "I suppose we should talk."

"I don't know if I want to talk to you. You didn't call me, remember?" Hurt doused my words.

"Right. That. You deserve an explanation."

"For what? Making out with me in the middle of a castle —no, two castles—and just leaving me hanging? For lying to me about having *the most enjoyable evening you have ever had* then not bothering to call when you said you would?" My exaggeration of his soft accent was terrible, but I was building steam. "It's been two weeks and I've heard nothing from you. Nothing. I actually believed you when you said you were a good guy. But clearly, you're the same jerk who spent a week giving me angry looks for absolutely no reason."

"I would hardly say I am a jerk."

"Really? Then what would you call making out with someone all night and then dropping off the face of the earth? You made me feel this big." I pinched my fingers together and held them just under his nose. "And where do you get off acting like that? What kind of scumbag just drops the cow once he gets a taste of the milk? Huh?"

"Would you be the cow in that scenario?"

"Don't mess with me right now," I threatened. "I called you. Because that's what nice people do when the person they like goes missing. They pick up the phone and call. I thought something horrible had happened to you. Was this whole thing just some ploy to see how far you could get with me?" The corner of Ull's mouth turned up in a smirk. *Seriously?* "Is this funny to you?"

The smirk broke into a full-fledged smile. "Are you finished?"

"Hardly." I glared into Ull's endless blue, traitor eyes.

"I did just save you," Ull reminded me.

"I had things under control."

"Oh, did you?"

"I was getting there."

"Right. Well, while you were getting there, I took care of the problem. The least you can do is let me explain." I thought about what I'd have been doing right now if Ull hadn't come along in the nightclub. Guilt stepped lightly on anger's toes.

"You know what?" I sighed, too exhausted to fight anymore. "I've had a long night. I just want to go home."

"Do you want to hear my explanation?"

"Do you think it'll make any difference?"

"Maybe."

"Maybe's not good enough." I turned and walked toward campus.

"This conversation is not over." Ull's voice was strained.

"Yes, it is. I get it. You weren't that into me. You're lousy at dumping girls. Case closed."

Ull grabbed my hand, forcing me to stop. "Please. It is not what you think."

I pulled my hand back and folded my arms. "It doesn't matter. I just want to go home." I resumed my brisk walk. Ull matched my pace.

"Fine. But this conversation is not over." He marched confidently beside me.

"Where exactly do you think you're going?"

"With you."

"No, you're not." I didn't care how good he looked in that coat; I was a woman of substance.

"I am making sure you get home safely, whether you like it or not. We can discuss this further tomorrow."

"I seriously doubt that," I muttered, picking up my pace in an effort to get away from him.

At that moment, Ull Myhr was the last person I wanted to be around.

Meet the Vikings (including Gunnar's Midgardian relative)
in VIKING ACADEMY!

When seventeen-year-old Saga Skånstad discovers an
antique dagger, she's sucked into a world where Vikings rule
the seas and dragons roam the skies, and the only thing more
dangerous than the chief who takes her captive is the rival
who steals her away.

Meet Gunnar's brother, Henrik, and Asgard's war god, Tyr, in PERFEKT ORDER.

All's fair when you're in love with War.

For seventeen-year-old Mia Ahlström, a world ruled by order is the only world she allows. A lifetime of chore charts, to-do lists and study schedules have helped earn her a spot at Redwood State University's engineering program. And while her five year plan includes finding her very own happily-evah-aftah, years at an all-girls boarding school left her feeling woefully unprepared for keg parties and co-ed extracurricular activities.

So nothing surprises her more than catching the eye of Tyr Fredriksen at her first college party. The imposing Swede is arrogantly charming, stubbornly overprotective, and runs hot-and-cold in ways that defy reason…until Mia learns that she's fallen for the Norse God of War; an immortal battle deity hiding on Midgard (Earth) to protect a valuable Asgardian treasure from a feral enemy. With a price on his head, Tyr brings more than a little excitement to Mia's rigidly controlled life. Choosing Tyr may be the biggest distraction—or the greatest adventure—she's ever had.

Learn more about the world of S.T. Bende at
www.stbende.com.

ACKNOWLEDGMENTS

An enormous thank you to the man who knows I hear Norse gods in my head and married me anyway. *Jeg elsker deg*. To our awe-inspiring boys, who fill our lives with faith, hope and love. You are the best thing that ever happened to us.

Takk to Stacey Nash, the most generous critique partner an author could have. *Tusen takk* to my writer friends; for reading drafts, sharing wisdom, and never letting me give up. And a huge thank you to *everyone* who offered advice and support along this journey.

And thanks to MorMorMa, for introducing me to these beautiful stories… and to Norsk waffles. *Takk for maten.*

Before finding domestic bliss in suburbia, internationally bestselling author S.T. Bende lived in Manhattan Beach (became overly fond of Peet's Coffee) and Europe…where she became overly fond of McVitie's cookies. Her love of Scandinavian culture and a very patient Norwegian teacher inspired her YA Norse fantasy books. And her love of a galaxy far, far away inspired her to write children's books for Star Wars. She hopes her characters make you smile, and she dreams of skiing on Jotunheim and Hoth.

Learn more about the world of S.T. Bende at
www.stbende.com.

www.ingramcontent.com/pod-product-compliance
Lightning Source LLC
Chambersburg PA
CBHW032052180726
48284CB00004B/1305